Fast and Slow

By Jack Challoner

Contents

Fast and Slow. 3
Moving Fast 4
Moving Slowly. 6
Measuring Speed 8
Speeding Up. 10
Slowing Down 12
Moving on Land 14
Moving in Water 16
Moving Through Air. 18
Fast Machines. 20
Moving in Space 22
Too Fast to See 24
Too Slow to See 26
Growing Fast and Slowly 28
Fastest and Slowest 30
Glossary and Index 32

Austin, Texas

© **Copyright 1997, text, Steck-Vaughn Company**

All rights reserved. No part of this book may be reproduced or utilized in any form or by any means, electronic or mechanical, including photocopying, recording, or by any information storage and retrieval system, without permission in writing from the Publisher. Inquiries should be addressed to:
Copyright Permissions, Steck-Vaughn Company, P.O. Box 26015, Austin, TX 78755

Published by Raintree Steck-Vaughn Publishers, an imprint of Steck-Vaughn Company

Editors: Kim Merlino, Kathy DeVico
Project Manager: Lyda Guz
Electronic Production: Scott Melcer

Photo Credits: cover: top Claire Paxton;
bottom Claire Paxton;
Robert Harding Picture Library: pp. 16, 30;
Frank Lane Photo Agency: p. 8 P. Perry; p. 13 Panda Photos;
NHPA: pp. 14, 17 Peter Parks; p. 19 Manfred Danegger;
p. 24 Stephen Dalton; p. 28 G. S. Bernard;
OSF: p. 15 R. Brown; p. 27 Avril Ranage; p. 29 G. Bernard;
SPL: p. 12 NASA; p. 22 NASA; p. 26 Stephen Dalton;
Tony Stone Images: pp. 4, 5 Colin Prior; p. 6 Schafer & Hill;
p. 10 William Hamilton; p. 18 P. Lamberti; p. 24 Randy Wells;
TRH: p. 23 NASA; Zefa: p. 3.
All other photographs by Claire Paxton.

Library of Congress Cataloging-in-Publication Data

Challoner, Jack.
Fast and slow / by Jack Challoner.
p. cm. — (Start-up science)
Includes index.
ISBN 0-8172-4320-8
1. Motion — Experiments — Juvenile literature. 2. Motion — Study and teaching (Elementary) — Activity programs — Juvenile literature. 3. Speed — Experiments — Juvenile literature. 4. Speed — Study and teaching (Elementary) — Activity programs — Juvenile literature.
[1. Motion — Experiments. 2. Speed — Experiments. 3. Experiments.]
I. Title. II. Series: Challoner, Jack. Start-up science.
QC133.5.C48 1997
531'.112 — dc20
95-50268
CIP
AC

Printed in Spain
Bound in the United States
1 2 3 4 5 6 7 8 9 0 LB 99 98 97 96

Fast and Slow

This book will answer lots of questions that you may have about fast and slow. But it will also make you think for yourself.

Each time you turn a page, you will find an activity that you can do yourself at home or at school. You may need help from an adult.

Why do some things happen very fast, while others take longer? Why can a train move faster than a bicycle? Why can a rocket move faster than a car?

Moving Fast

Sometimes it is important for you to move a long distance in a short time. To do this, you must move fast. Can you think of some things that move fast?

Did you know?

Another word for fast is rapid. Water moves very fast in parts of rivers. These parts are called **rapids**.

Winning a race

In a race, the fastest person usually wins. The people in this race have to push their wheels to move along. The harder they push, the faster they will go.

Fast animals

These giraffes usually walk slowly on their long legs. But they can run very fast if they are chased by a lion.

Now try this

One way to make things go fast is to roll them down a slope.

You will need:

a marble, a tray or a large piece of cardboard

1. Hold one end of the tray above the table to make a slope.

2. Roll the marble down the slope. Do not push the marble. Does the marble go faster or slower if you make the slope higher?

Moving Slowly

Things that move slowly take a long time to go a short distance. Children who are just learning to walk move more slowly than adults do when they walk.

Did you know?

Some people have slow bicycle races. The idea is to ride your bicycle as slowly as possible, without falling off of it.

Slow walker

This baby is learning to walk. To begin with, she takes small steps and moves very slowly. As she grows older, she will take bigger, faster steps.

Heavy and slow

This tortoise moves very slowly. It does not need to move fast, because it has a strong shell to protect it from **predators**.

Now try this

People who walk slowly do not move as far in the same amount of time as people who walk quickly.

You will need:
a friend

1. Stand next to your friend in a large room or outdoors.

2. Now both walk forward at the same time. You should walk slowly, while your friend walks more quickly.

3. Walk for about ten seconds, and see who has moved farther.

Measuring Speed

The **speed** of something tells you how fast it is moving. A car moving at a steady speed of 25 miles (40 km) per hour would travel 25 miles (40 km) in an hour.

How fast?

This herd of zebras walks about 3 miles (5 km) every hour. This means that the speed of the herd is 3 miles (5 km) per hour.

Did you know?

Borzoi dogs can run very fast. They were bred to hunt wolves in Russia. Borzoi means "speed" in Russian.

How long?

This is a stopwatch. It is being used to measure how long a sprinter takes to run 200 meters. The faster the sprinter runs, the less time she will take.

Now try this

A **speedometer** shows how fast a car moves. You can make a speedometer of your own.

You will need:
a piece of paper 6 inches x 1 inch (15 cm x 2 cm), a drinking straw, tape, a bamboo skewer

1. Tape the paper to the straw so that it hangs down. Push the skewer through the straw.

2. Hold one end of the skewer, and walk. What happens to the paper as you move faster? Slower?

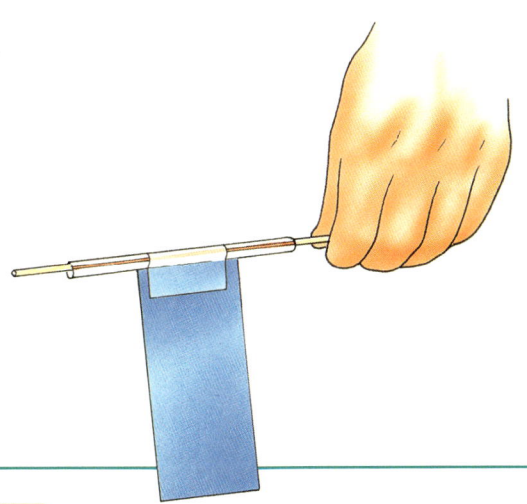

BE SAFE!
Skewers have a pointed end.

Speeding Up

Whenever something moves faster, it speeds up. It needs a push or a pull to do this. When things move downhill, they speed up. It is **gravity** that pulls them down the hill.

Did you know?

Downhill skiers can reach speeds of more than 62 miles (100 km) per hour as gravity pulls them downhill.

Push it!

These people are pushing a bobsled to make it go faster. Once it is moving, the people will jump inside the bobsled, and it will slide very fast on the ice.

Faster and faster

As it moves downhill, this bicycle moves faster and faster. It is pulled down the hill by gravity. At the bottom, the rider must use the **brakes** to slow down.

Now try this

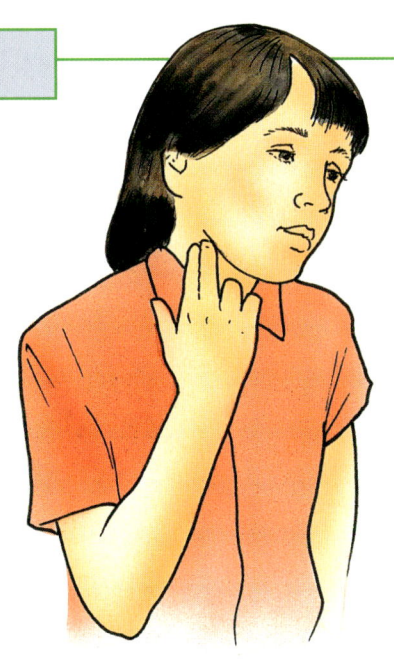

When you exercise, your heartbeat speeds up.

1. Place two fingers on the side of your throat, near the front, as shown.

2. You should feel a movement every time your heart beats.

3. Run or skip around for a few minutes. Feel your pulse again. Is it faster or slower?

Slowing Down

How can you make something slow down? If it is a car or a bicycle, you simply use the brakes. Most things slow down when they rub against other things.

Air brakes

Did you know?

Brakes on a bicycle pull on the wheels by rubbing against them. This helps to stop the bicycle.

This is a space shuttle. It moves very fast. To slow down, the pilot uses a **parachute**. The parachute pulls on the shuttle and slows it down.

Large wings

To slow down, birds hold out their wings. The wings act like parachutes and slow the bird's speed.

Now try this

A bicycle has brakes to slow it down. You can see how the brakes work.

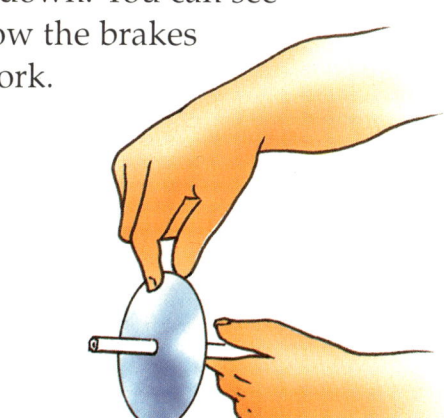

You will need:
a pencil, a circle of cardboard about 4 inches (10 cm) across

1. Ask an adult to push the pencil through the middle of the cardboard.

2. Hold the pencil in one hand, and spin the cardboard with the other.

3. Grasp the spinning cardboard gently with a finger and thumb. It will slow down.

Moving on Land

A car needs an engine to start it moving, and to keep it going. In the same way, fast animals must have strong muscles in their arms and legs to push themselves along.

Did you know?

At full speed, an emu can run as fast as the fastest athlete, about 28 miles (45 km) per hour.

Big jumper

Kangaroos move across land quickly in huge jumps. Some jumps are as long as 39 feet (12 m).

Long legs

Unlike most birds, this emu cannot fly. Instead, it runs quickly along the ground on its long, strong legs.

Now try this

Find out how far you can jump.

You will need:
a tape measure,
a short, straight stick

1. Place the stick on the grass, and stand behind it.

2. Jump as far forward as you can, and stand still.

3. Ask an adult to measure the distance from the stick to your feet. How far did you jump?

Moving in Water

If you have ever tried to walk quickly through the shallow end of a swimming pool, you know that it is quite difficult. Animals that live in water have many different ways of moving around quickly.

Fast swimmer

Seals like this one need to swim fast to catch fish. Their **streamlined** shape and powerful tail mean that they can swim fast underwater.

Did you know?

One of the fastest animals in water is the flying fish. When it is moving fast, it sometimes leaps up out of the water into the air.

Swimming slowly

This jellyfish spends much of its time drifting along in the water. It feeds on tiny sea creatures that drift toward it.

Now try this

Streamlined shapes move more quickly through water than other shapes.

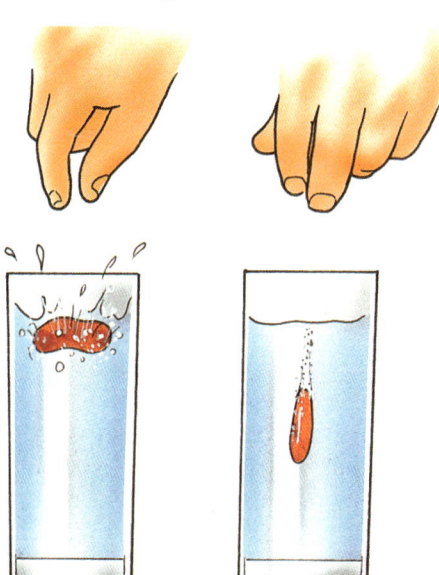

You will need:

two tall glasses, water, modeling clay

1. Break off two small lumps of modeling clay. Make one smooth and pointed, and make the other a very rough shape.

2. Fill both of the glasses almost to the top with water.

3. Drop both shapes, one into each glass of water, at the same time. Which shape moves faster?

Moving Through Air

Most birds fly through the air by flapping their wings. Birds use their wings to go faster and slower, or to change direction.

Did you know?

The spine-tailed swift can fly at a speed of about 100 miles (160 km) per hour, faster than many cars travel.

Falling slowly

At the start of a jump out of an airplane, you fall faster and faster. But when the parachute opens, it slows your speed.

Faster and faster

Large birds have to move fast before they can take off. Swans use their webbed feet to move over the water fast.

Now try this

Make your own parachute.

You will need:

modeling clay, a handkerchief, four 8-inch (20-cm) pieces of string

1. Tie one end of each piece of string to a corner of the handkerchief.

2. Press the free ends of the string into the modeling clay.

3. Stand on a chair, and hold two corners of the handkerchief. Let go of the parachute.

Fast Machines

People have made machines that travel on land, in water, and in the air. Fast-moving machines must have powerful engines. Most of these fast machines also have a streamlined shape.

Did you know?

The huge engines of a jumbo jet push it through the air at a high speed. A jet's high speed is what keeps it in the air.

Fast car

Look at the shape of this car. As it moves along the road, air passes easily over it. This allows it to move very fast.

Motorboat

Nearly all boats are pointed at the front. This makes them more streamlined. It helps them to move at high speeds through the water.

Now try this

You can see for yourself how a streamlined shape helps you move faster.

You will need:
a large umbrella

1. Open the umbrella, and hold it out in front of you.

2. Move forward as quickly as you can.

3. Close the umbrella, and try again. Is it easier to move now?

Moving in Space

In space there is no air, so things do not need to be streamlined to move fast.

To get into space, we need powerful rockets. Rockets can travel very fast.

Moonwalking

Astronauts walk on the moon with large, slow steps. They weigh less on the moon than they do on Earth. So their feet do not fall as quickly to the ground after each step.

Did you know?

Meteors are lumps of rock and dust that move very fast through space. When they meet the air around the Earth, most of them burn up.

Liftoff

Rockets like this one need to travel more than 7 miles (11 km) every second to get into space.

Now try this

You can make your own rocket.

You will need:
a long balloon,
tape, a drinking straw,
a long piece of string,
a chair

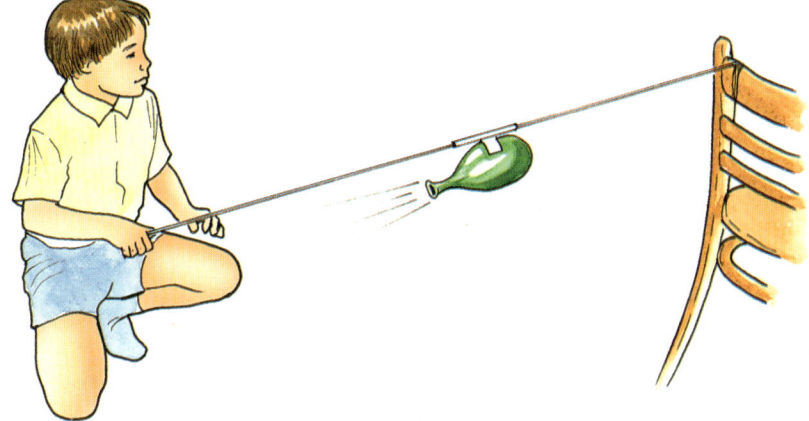

1. Push the string through a 4-inch (10-cm) piece of straw. Tie one end of the string to a chair.

2. Blow up the balloon, and hold the end closed.

3. Tape the balloon to the straw as shown in the picture.

4. Pull the string tight, and bring the balloon to the free end of the string. Let go of the balloon.

Too Fast to See

Our eyes can see many things. But some things happen too fast for us to see. Special photographs can show us what happened.

Did you know?

Chameleons catch flies on their tongues. The tongue moves too quickly for us to see without a special camera.

Fast wings

A bee's wings flap so fast that they appear to be just a blur. But in this special photograph, you can see the bee's wings clearly.

Moving pictures

When you watch a film, you are actually seeing many separate pictures. They are shown quickly, one after the other. The pictures change so fast that they seem to move.

Now try this

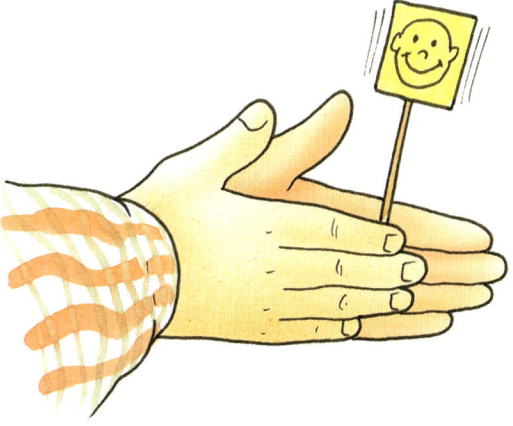

You can see how very fast things can blur together.

You will need:

a square piece of cardboard, a pencil, tape

1. Draw the outline of a head in the middle of one side of the cardboard.

2. In the middle of the other side of the cardboard, draw a mouth, a nose, and eyes.

3. Tape the cardboard to the pencil. Now hold the pencil between your hands, and rub it back and forth quickly. You should see the whole face.

Too Slow to See

Some things happen so slowly that you do not notice them for a time. For example, you cannot see a plant growing, but you know that it happens.

Did you know?

The stars seem to move across the sky very slowly during the night. This is because the Earth is spinning.

Making a valley

A valley like this one takes millions of years to form. The land moves and changes very slowly, as the weather and the river gradually wear the rock away.

Rotten apple

Many foods, such as this apple, become rotten very slowly. The last of these photographs was taken several weeks after the first one was taken.

Now try this

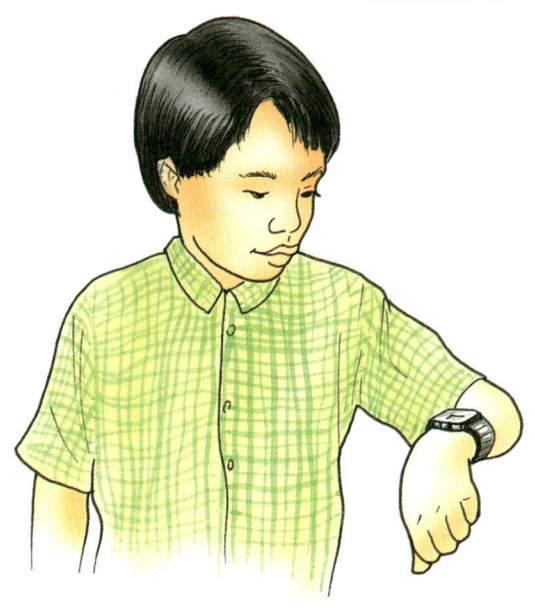

The minute hand of a clock moves too slowly for you to see. But you can see that it has moved after a few minutes.

You will need:
a clock or watch with a minute hand (the long hand)

1. Watch the minute hand. Can you see it move?

2. Keep watching it for a few minutes. You will see that it has moved from where it was.

Growing Fast and Slowly

Most plants and animals, including you, only grow a little bit every day. Young creatures grow very fast. A seed also grows quickly to become a young plant.

Did you know?

A starfish can slowly grow back parts of its body that have either been lost or damaged.

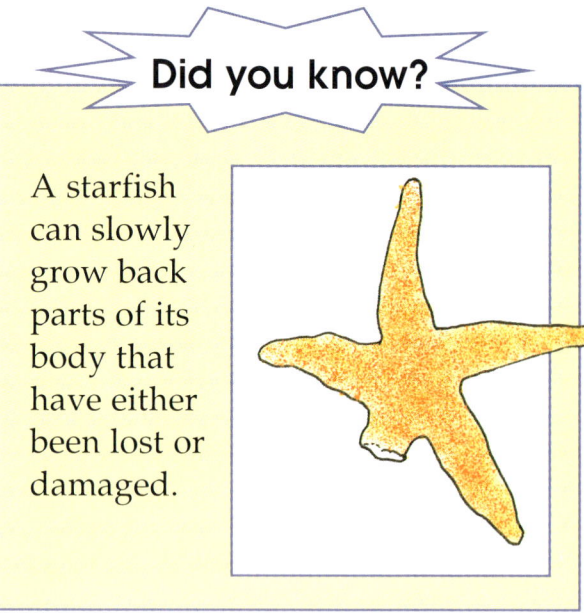

Tall grass

Bamboo is a type of grass. It can grow taller than a house. Bamboo can also grow very fast—as much as 12 inches (30 cm) every day.

Growing up fast

Young rabbits grow very fast. The newborn rabbits shown above only take five weeks to grow to the size of the rabbit on the right.

Now try this

You grow a little bit every day. You can measure this for yourself.

You will need:
a pencil, a wall or doorway that you are allowed to write on

1. Take off your shoes, and stand with your back against the wall.

2. Ask an older friend to mark your height and the date on the wall.

3. If you do this every three months, you will be able to see how fast or slowly you are growing.

Fastest and Slowest

The cheetah and the snail are the fastest and the slowest animals that live on land. A cheetah can catch any animal it wants to eat. A snail has a hard shell to protect it from predators.

Did you know?

Nothing can move faster than light. When you turn on a flashlight, it sends out light at a very high speed.

Fast runner

The cheetah is the fastest of all animals. It travels at speeds of up to 68 miles (110 km) per hour.

Slow snails

Snails move very slowly. These snails would take over an hour to move just a few yards.

Now try this

See how long it takes you to run 100 meters.

You will need:
a stopwatch, a friend

1. Ask an adult to mark a distance of about 100 meters.

2. Ask the adult to start the stopwatch when you start running and to stop it when you have run 100 meters. Have your friend run it next.

3. How long did it take each of you to run 100 meters? Which one of you ran the faster time?

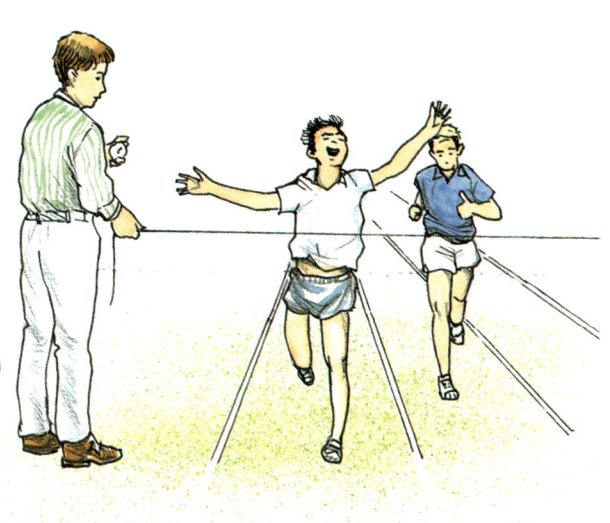

Glossary

brakes Brakes stop or slow a moving vehicle by keeping the wheels from turning.

gravity A force that pulls objects toward one another. Earth's gravity pulls a ball down to the ground.

meteors Lumps of rock or dust traveling in outer space

parachute A large piece of cloth that slows down a falling or fast-moving object.

predators Animals that catch and kill other animals for food

rapids Parts of a river where the water flows very quickly

speed The rate at which an object is moving

speedometer A device that measures the speed of a vehicle

streamlined Having a smooth shape that moves easily through air or water

Index

animals 5, 7, 8, 13, 14–15, 16–17, 18–19, 24, 28–29, 30–31

bamboo 28
bees 24
bicycle 3, 6, 11, 12, 13
birds 13, 15, 18, 19
boats 21
bobsled 10
borzoi dog 8
brakes 11, 12, 13

car 8, 9, 20, 30
chameleon 24
cheetah 30
clock 27

Earth 22, 26
emu 14, 15

flying fish 16

giraffe 5

gravity 10–11

jellyfish 17

kangaroo 14

light 30

meteors 22
moon 22

parachute 12, 18–19
plants 26, 28
predators 7, 30
pulse 11

rabbits 29
race 4, 6
rivers 4, 26
rockets 22–23
rotting 27

seals 16
skiers 10

snails 30–31
space 22–23
space shuttle 12
speed 8–9
speedometer 9
starfish 28
stars 26
stopwatch 9
streamlined 16, 17, 20–21, 22
swan 19
swift, spine-tailed 18
swimming pool 16

tortoise 6
trains 3

walking 6–7

zebras 8

© 1996 Belitha Press Ltd.